Life everin elsey
I was Se
for a

Self"
To
Heuy my
Soul on
Until
it
was
Ready
Redi fa what? →

'We were friends, somehow. But in the end, somehow, he intended to be a mortal enemy. All the while that he was making the gestures of a close and precious friend he was fattening my soul in a coop till it was ready for killing'

SAUL BELLOW
Born 10 June 1915, Montreal, Quebec
Died 5 April 2005, Brookline, Massachusetts

'Him With His Foot in His Mouth' first published in book
form in *Him With His Foot in His Mouth and Other Stories*,
New York 1984 and included in the *Collected Stories*, 2001.

ALSO PUBLISHED BY PENGUIN BOOKS
*Dangling Man · The Victim · The Adventures of Augie
March · Seize the Day · Henderson the Rain King · Herzog ·
Mr Sammler's Planet · Humboldt's Gift · To Jerusalem
and Back · The Dean's December · More Die of
Heartbreak · The Actual · Ravelstein · Collected Stories*

SAUL BELLOW

Him With His Foot
in His Mouth

PENGUIN BOOKS

PENGUIN CLASSICS

Published by the Penguin Group
Penguin Books Ltd, 80 Strand, London WC2R 0RL, England
Penguin Group (USA), Inc., 375 Hudson Street, New York, New York 10014, USA
Penguin Group (Canada), 90 Eglinton Avenue East, Suite 700, Toronto, Ontario,
Canada M4P 2Y3 (a division of Pearson Penguin Canada Inc.)
Penguin Ireland, 25 St Stephen's Green, Dublin 2, Ireland (a division of Penguin Books Ltd)
Penguin Group (Australia), 250 Camberwell Road, Camberwell, Victoria 3124, Australia
(a division of Pearson Australia Group Pty Ltd)
Penguin Books India Pvt Ltd, 11 Community Centre, Panchsheel Park,
New Delhi – 110 017, India
Penguin Group (NZ), 67 Apollo Drive, Rosedale, North Shore 0632, New Zealand
(a division of Pearson New Zealand Ltd)
Penguin Books (South Africa) (Pty) Ltd, 24 Sturdee Avenue, Rosebank, Johannesburg 2196,
South Africa

Penguin Books Ltd, Registered Offices: 80 Strand, London WC2R 0RL, England

www.penguin.com

Selected from *Collected Stories* published in Penguin Classics 2007
This edition published in Penguin Classics 2011
3

Copyright © Saul Bellow, 2001

Typeset by Jouve (UK), Milton Keynes
Printed in England by Clays Ltd, St Ives plc

ISBN: 978-0-141-19574-2

www.greenpenguin.co.uk

Penguin Books is committed to a sustainable future
for our business, our readers and our planet.
The book in your hands is made from paper
certified by the Forest Stewardship Council.

Him With His Foot in His Mouth

Dear Miss Rose: I almost began 'My Dear Child,' because in a sense what I did to you thirty-five years ago makes us the children of each other. I have from time to time remembered that I long ago made a bad joke at your expense and have felt uneasy about it, but it was spelled out to me recently that what I said to you was so wicked, so lousy, gross, insulting, unfeeling, and savage that you could never in a thousand years get over it. I wounded you for life, so I am given to understand, and I am the more greatly to blame because this attack was so gratuitous. We had met in passing only, we scarcely knew each other. Now, the person who charges me with this cruelty is not without prejudice toward me, he is out to get me, obviously. Nevertheless, I have been in a tizzy since reading his accusations. I wasn't exactly in great shape when his letter arrived. Like many elderly men, I have to swallow all sorts of pills. I take Inderal and quinidine for hypertension and cardiac disorders, and I am also, for a variety of psychological reasons, deeply distressed and for the moment without ego defenses.

It may give more substance to my motive in writing to you now if I tell you that for some months I have been visiting an old woman who reads Swedenborg and other occult authors. She tells me (and a man in his sixties can't easily close his mind to such suggestions) that there is a life to come – wait and see – and that in the life to come we will feel the pains that we inflicted on others. We will suffer all that we made them suffer, for after death all experience is reversed. We enter into the souls of those whom we knew in life. They enter also into us and feel and judge us from within. On the outside chance that this old Canadian woman has it right, I must try to take up this matter with you. It's not as though I had tried to murder you, but my offense is palpable all the same.

I will say it all and then revise, send Miss Rose only the suitable parts.

. . . In this life between birth and death, while it is still possible to make amends . . .

I wonder whether you remember me at all, other than as the person who wounded you – a tall man and, in those days, dark on the whole, with a mustache (not worn thick), physically a singular individual, a touch of the camel about him, something amusing in his composition. If you can recall the Shawmut of those days, you should see him now. *Edad con Sus Disgracias* is the title Goya gave to the etching of an old man who struggles to rise from the chamber pot, his pants dropped to his ankles. 'Together with most weak hams,' as Hamlet wickedly says to Polonius, being merciless about old men. To the disorders aforementioned I must add teeth with cracked roots, periodontia requiring antibiotics that gave me the runs and resulted in a hemorrhoid the size of a walnut, plus creeping arthritis of the hands. Winter is gloomy and wet in British Columbia, and when I awoke one morning in this land of exile from which I face extradition, I discovered that something had gone wrong with the middle finger of the right hand. The hinge had stopped working and the finger was curled like a snail – a painful new affliction. Quite a joke on me. And the extradition is real. I have been served with papers.

So at the very least I can try to reduce the torments of the afterlife by one.

It may appear that I come groveling with hard-luck stories after thirty-five years, but as you will see, such is not the case.

I traced you through Miss Da Sousa at Ribier College, where we were all colleagues in the late forties.

3

She has remained there, in Massachusetts, where so much of the nineteenth century still stands, and she wrote to me when my embarrassing and foolish troubles were printed in the papers. She is a kindly, intelligent woman who *like yourself, should I say that?* never married. Answering with gratitude, I asked what had become of you and was told that you were a retired librarian living in Orlando, Florida.

I never thought that I would envy people who had retired, but that was when retirement was still an option. For me it's not in the cards now. The death of my brother leaves me in a deep legal-financial hole. I won't molest you with the facts of the case, garbled in the newspapers. Enough to say that his felonies and my own faults or vices have wiped me out. On bad legal advice I took refuge in Canada, and the courts will be rough because I tried to escape. I may not be sent to prison, but I will have to work for the rest of my natural life, will die in harness, and damn queer harness, hauling my load to a peculiar peak. One of my father's favorite parables was about a feeble horse flogged cruelly by its driver. A bystander tries to intercede: 'The load is too heavy, the hill is steep, it's useless to beat your old horse on the face, why do you do it?' 'To be a horse was *his* idea,' the driver says.

I have a lifelong weakness for this sort of Jewish

humor, which may be alien to you not only because you are Scotch-Irish (so Miss Da Sousa says) but also because you as a (pre-computer) librarian were in another sphere – zone of quiet, within the circumference of the Dewey decimal system. It is possible that you may have disliked the life of a nun or shepherdess which the word 'librarian' once suggested. You may resent it for keeping you out of the modern 'action' – erotic, narcotic, dramatic, dangerous, salty. Maybe you have loathed circulating other people's lawless raptures, handling wicked books (for the most part fake, take it from me, Miss Rose). Allow me to presume that you are old-fashioned enough not to be furious at having led a useful life. If you aren't an old-fashioned person I haven't hurt you so badly after all. No modern woman would brood for forty years over a stupid wisecrack. She would say, 'Get lost!'

Who is it that accuses me of having wounded you? Eddie Walish, that's who. He has become the main planner of college humanities surveys in the State of Missouri, I am given to understand. At such work he is wonderful, a man of genius. But although he now lives in Missouri, he seems to think of nothing but Massachusetts in the old days. He can't forget the evil I did. He was there when I did it (whatever *it* really was), and he writes, 'I have to remind you of how you hurt Carla

5

Rose. So characteristic of you, when she was trying to be agreeable, not just to miss her gentle intentions but to give her a shattering kick in the face. I happen to know that you traumatized her for life.' (Notice how the liberal American vocabulary is used as a torture device: By 'characteristic' he means: 'You are not a *good person*, Shawmut.') Now, were you really traumatized, Miss Rose? How does Walish 'happen to know'? Did you tell him? Or is it, as I conjecture, nothing but gossip? I wonder if you remember the occasion at all. It would be a mercy if you didn't. And I don't want to thrust unwanted recollections on you, but if I did indeed disfigure you so cruelly, is there any way to avoid remembering?

So let's go back again to Ribier College. Walish and I were great friends then, young instructors, he in literature, I in fine arts – my specialty music history. As if this were news to you; my book on Pergolesi is in all libraries. Impossible that you shouldn't have come across it. Besides, I've done those musicology programs on public television, which were quite popular.

But we are back in the forties. The term began just after Labor Day. My first teaching position. After seven or eight weeks I was still wildly excited. Let me start with the beautiful New England setting. Fresh from

Chicago and from Bloomington, Indiana, where I took my degree, I had never seen birches, roadside ferns, deep pinewoods, little white steeples. What could I be but out of place? It made me scream with laughter to be called 'Dr Shawmut.' I felt absurd here, a camel on the village green. I am a high-waisted and long-legged man, who is susceptible to paradoxical, ludicrous images of himself. I hadn't yet gotten the real picture of Ribier, either. It wasn't true New England, it was a bohemian college for rich kids from New York who were too nervous for the better schools, unadjusted.

Now then: Eddie Walish and I walking together past the college library. Sweet autumnal warmth against a background of chill from the surrounding woods – it's all there for me. The library is a Greek Revival building and the light in the porch is mossy and sunny – bright-green moss, leafy sunlight, lichen on the columns. I am turned on, manic, flying. My relations with Walish at this stage are easy to describe: very cheerful, not a kink in sight, not a touch of darkness. I am keen to learn from him, because I have never seen a progressive college, never lived in the East, never come in contact with the Eastern Establishment, of which I have heard so much. What is it all about? A girl to whom I was assigned as adviser has asked for another one because I haven't been psycho-analyzed and can't even begin to relate to her. And this very morning I have spent two hours in a committee meeting to determine whether a course in history should be obligatory for fine-arts majors. Tony Lemnitzer, professor of painting, said, 'Let the kids read about the kings and the queens – what can it hoit them?' Brooklyn Tony, who had run away from home to be a circus roustabout, became a poster artist and eventually an Abstract Expressionist. 'Don't ever feel sorry for Tony,' Walish advises me. 'The woman he married is a millionairess. She's built him a studio fit for Michelangelo. He's embarrassed to paint, he only whittles there. He carved out two wooden balls inside a bird-cage.' Walish himself, Early Hip with a Harvard background, suspected at first that my ignorance was a put-on. A limping short man, Walish looked at me – looked upward – with real shrewdness and traces of disbelief about the mouth. From Chicago, a Ph.D. out of Bloomington, Indiana, can I be as backward as I seem? But I am good company, and by and by he tells me (is it a secret?) that although he comes from Gloucester, Mass., he's not a real Yankee. His father, a second-generation American, is a machinist, retired, uneducated. One of the old man's letters reads, 'Your poor mother – the doctor says she has a groweth on her virginia which he will have to operate. When she goes to surgery I expect you and your sister to be here to stand by me.'

There were two limping men in the community, and their names were similar. The other limper, Edmund Welch, justice of the peace, walked with a cane. Our Ed, who suffered from curvature of the spine, would not carry a stick, much less wear a built-up shoe. He behaved with sporting nonchalance and defied the orthopedists when they warned that his spinal column would collapse like a stack of dominoes. His style was to be free and limber. You had to take him as he came, no concessions offered. I admired him for that.

Now, Miss Rose, you have come out of the library for a breath of air and are leaning, arms crossed, and resting your head against a Greek column. To give himself more height, Walish wears his hair thick. You couldn't cram a hat over it. But I have on a baseball cap. Then, Miss Rose, you say, smiling at me, 'Oh, Dr Shawmut, in that cap you look like an archaeologist.' Before I can stop myself, I answer, 'And you look like something I just dug up.'

Awful!

The pair of us, Walish and I, hurried on. Eddie, whose hips were out of line, made an effort to walk more quickly, and when we were beyond your little library temple I saw that he was grinning at me, his warm face looking up into my face with joy, with accusing admiration. He had witnessed something extraordinary. What

9

this something might be, whether it came under the heading of fun or psychopathology or wickedness, nobody could yet judge, but he was glad. Although he lost no time in clearing himself of guilt, it was exactly his kind of wisecrack. He loved to do the Groucho Marx bit, or give an S. J. Perelman turn to his sentences. As for me, I had become dead sober, as I generally do after making one of my cracks. I am as astonished by them as anybody else. They may be hysterical symptoms, in the clinical sense. I used to consider myself absolutely normal, but I became aware long ago that in certain moods my laughing bordered on hysteria. I myself could hear the abnormal note. Walish knew very well that I was subject to such seizures, and when he sensed that one of my fits was approaching, he egged me on. And after he had had his fun he would say, with a grin like Pan Satyrus, 'What a bastard you are, Shawmut. The sadistic stabs you can give!' He took care, you see, not to be incriminated as an accessory.

And my joke wasn't even witty, just vile, no excuse for it, certainly not 'inspiration.' Why should inspiration be so idiotic? It was simply idiotic and wicked. Walish used to tell me, 'You're a Surrealist in spite of yourself.' His interpretation was that I had raised myself by painful efforts from immigrant origins to a middle-class level but that I avenged myself for the torments and falsifications of my healthy instincts, deformities imposed on me by this adaptation to respectability, the strain of social climbing. Clever, intricate analysis of this sort was popular in Greenwich Village at that time, and Walish had picked up the habit. His letter of last month was filled with insights of this kind. People seldom give up the mental capital accumulated in their 'best' years. At sixty-odd, Eddie is still a youthful Villager and associates with young people, mainly. I have accepted old age.

It isn't easy to write with arthritic fingers. My lawyer, whose fatal advice I followed (he is the youngest brother of my wife, who passed away last year), urged me to go to British Columbia, where, because of the Japanese current, flowers grow in midwinter, and the air is purer. There are indeed primroses out in the snow, but my hands are crippled and I am afraid that I may have to take gold injections if they don't improve. Nevertheless, I build up the fire and sit concentrating in the rocker because I need to make it worth your while to consider these facts with me. If I am to believe Walish, you have trembled from that day onward like a flame on a middle-class altar of undeserved humiliation. One of the insulted and injured.

From my side I have to admit that it was hard for me to acquire decent manners, not because I was naturally rude but because I felt the strain of my position. I came to believe for a time that I couldn't get on in life until I, too, had a false self like everybody else and so I made special efforts to be considerate, deferential, civil. And of course I overdid things and wiped myself twice where people of better breeding only wiped once. But no such program of betterment could hold me for long. I set it up, and then I tore it down, and burned it in a raging bonfire.

Walish, I must tell you, gives me the business in his letter. Why was it, he asks, that when people groped in conversations I supplied the missing phrases and finished their sentences with greedy pedantry? Walish alleges that I was showing off, shuffling out of my vulgar origins, making up to the genteel and qualifying as the kind of Jew acceptable (just barely) to the Christian society of T. S. Eliot's dreams. Walish pictures me as an upwardly mobile pariah seeking bondage as one would seek salvation. In reaction, he says, I had rebellious fits and became wildly insulting. Walish notes all this well, but he did not come out with it during the years when we were close. He saved it all up. At Ribier College we liked each other. We were friends, somehow. But in the end, somehow, he intended to be a mortal enemy. All the while that he was making the gestures of a close and precious friend he was fattening my soul in a coop

till it was ready for killing. My success in musicology
may have been too much for him.

Eddie told his wife – he told everyone – what I had
said to you. It certainly got around the campus. People
laughed, but I was depressed. Remorse: you were a pale
woman with thin arms, absorbing the colors of moss,
lichen, and limestone into your skin. The heavy library
doors were open, and within there were green reading
lamps and polished heavy tables, and books massed up
to the gallery and above. A few of these books were
exalted, some were usefully informative, the majority
of them would only congest the mind. My Swedenbor-
gian old lady says that angels do not read books. Why
should they? Nor, I imagine, can librarians be great
readers. They have too many books, most of them bur-
densome. The crowded shelves give off an inviting,
consoling, seductive odor that is also tinctured faintly
with something pernicious, with poison and doom.
Human beings can lose their lives in libraries. They
ought to be warned. And you, an underpriestess of this
temple stepping out to look at the sky, and Mr Lubeck,
your chief, a gentle refugee always stumbling over his
big senile dog and apologizing to the animal, 'Ach,
excuse me!' (heavy on the sibilant).

*Personal note: Miss Rose never was pretty, not even what
the French call* une belle laide, *or ugly beauty, a woman*

whose command of sexual forces makes ugliness itself con-
tribute to her erotic power. A belle laide (it would be a
French idea!) has to be a rolling-mill of lusts. Such force was
lacking. No organic basis for it. Fifty years earlier Miss Rose
would have been taking Lydia Pinkham's Vegetable Com-
pound. Nevertheless, even if she looked green, a man might
have loved her – loved her for her timid warmth, or for the
courage she had had to muster to compliment me on my cap.
Thirty-five years ago I might have bluffed out this embarrass-
ment with compliments, saying, 'Only think, Miss Rose,
how many objects of rare beauty have been dug up by
archaeologists – the Venus de Milo, Assyrian winged bulls
with the faces of great kings. And Michelangelo even buried
one of his statues to get the antique look and then exhumed
it.' But it's too late for rhetorical gallantries. I'd be ashamed.
Unpretty, unmarried, the nasty little community laughing at
my crack, Miss Rose, poor thing, must have been in despair.

Eddie Walish, as I told you, would not act the cripple
despite his spiral back. Even though he slouched and
walked with an outslapping left foot, he carried himself
with style. He wore good English tweeds and Lloyd &
Haig brogans. He himself would say that there were
enough masochistic women around to encourage any
fellow to preen and cut a figure. Handicapped men did
very well with girls of a certain type. You, Miss Rose,
would have done better to save your compliment for

him. But his wife was then expecting; I was the bachelor.

Almost daily during the first sunny days of the term we went out walking. I found him mysterious then.

I would think: Who is he, anyway, this (suddenly) close friend of mine? What is this strange figure, the big head low beside me, whose hair grows high and thick? With a different slant, like whipcord stripes, it grows thickly also from his ears. One of the campus ladies has suggested that I urge him to shave his ears, but why should I? She wouldn't like him better with shaven ears, she only dreams that she might. He has a sort of woodwind laugh, closer to oboe than to clarinet, and he releases his laugh from the wide end of his nose as well as from his carved pumpkin mouth. He grins like Alfred E. Neuman from the cover of *Mad* magazine, the successor to Peck's Bad Boy. His eyes, however, are warm and induce me to move closer and closer, but they withhold what I want most. I long for his affection, I distrust him and love him, I woo him with wisecracks. For he is a wise guy in an up-to-date postmodern existentialist sly manner. He also seems kindly. He seems all sorts of things. Fond of Brecht and Weill, he sings 'Mackie Messer' and trounces out the tune on the upright piano. This, however, is merely period stuff – German cabaret jazz of the twenties, Berlin's answer to trench warfare and exploded humanism. Catch Eddie allowing himself to be dated like that! Up-to-the-minute Eddie has always been in the avant-garde. An early fan of the Beat poets, he was the first to quote me Allen Ginsberg's wonderful line 'America I'm putting my queer shoulder to the wheel.'

Eddie made me an appreciative reader of Ginsberg, from whom I learned much about wit. You may find it odd, Miss Rose (I myself do), that I should have kept up with Ginsberg from way back. Allow me, however, to offer a specimen statement from one of his recent books, which is memorable and also charming. Ginsberg writes that Walt Whitman slept with Edward Carpenter, the author of *Love's Coming-of-Age*; Carpenter afterward became the lover of the grandson of one of our obscurer presidents, Chester A. Arthur; Gavin Arthur when he was very old was the lover of a San Francisco homosexual who, when he embraced Ginsberg, completed the entire cycle and brought the Sage of Camden in touch with his only true successor and heir. It's all a little like Dr Pangloss's account of how he came to be infected with syphilis.

Please forgive this, Miss Rose. It seems to me that we will need the broadest possible human background for this inquiry, which may so much affect your emotions and mine. You ought to know to whom you were speaking on that day when you got up your nerve, smiling and trembling, to pay me a compliment – to give me, us, your blessing. Which I repaid with a bad witticism drawn, characteristically, from the depths of my nature, that hoard of strange formulations. I had almost forgotten the event when Walish's letter reached me in Canada. That letter – a strange *megillah* of which I myself was the Haman. He must have brooded with *ressentiment* for decades on my character, drawing the profile of my inmost soul over and over and over. He compiled a list of all my faults, my sins, and the particulars are so fine, the inventory so extensive, the summary so condensed, that he must have been collecting, filing, formulating, and polishing furiously throughout the warmest, goldenest days of our friendship. To receive such a document – I ask you to imagine, Miss Rose, how it affected me at a time when I was coping with grief and gross wrongs, mourning my wife (and funnily enough, also my swindling brother), and experiencing *Edad con Sus Disgracias*, discovering that I could no longer straighten my middle finger, reckoning up the labor and sorrow of threescore and ten (rapidly approaching). At our age, my dear, nobody can be indignant or surprised when evil is manifested, but I ask myself again and again, why should Eddie Walish work up my faults for thirty-some years to cast them into my teeth? This is what excites my keenest interest, so keen it makes me scream inwardly. The whole comedy of it comes over me in the night with the intensity of labor pains. I lie in the back bedroom of this little box of a Canadian house, which is scarcely insulated, and bear down hard so as not to holler. All the neighbors need is to hear such noises at three in the morning. And there isn't a soul in British Columbia I can discuss this with. My only acquaintance is Mrs Gracewell, the old woman (she is very old) who studies occult literature, and I can't bother her with so different a branch of experience. Our conversations are entirely theoretical . . . One helpful remark she did make, and this was: 'The lower self is what the Psalmist referred to when he wrote, "I am a worm and no man." The higher self, few people are equipped to observe. This is the reason they speak so unkindly of one another.'

More than once Walish's document (denunciation) took off from Ginsberg's poetry and prose, and so I finally sent an order to City Lights in San Francisco and have spent many evenings studying books of his I had missed – he publishes so many tiny ones. Ginsberg takes a stand for true tenderness and full candor. Real candor means excremental and genital literalness. What Ginsberg opts for is the warmth of a freely copulating, manly, womanly, comradely, 'open road' humanity which doesn't neglect to pray and to meditate. He speaks with horror of our 'plastic culture,' which he connects somewhat obsessively with the CIA. And in addition to the CIA there are other spydoms, linked with Exxon, Mobil, Standard Oil of California, sinister Occidental Petroleum with its Kremlin connections (that *is* a weird one to contemplate, undeniably). Supercapitalism and its carcinogenic petrochemical technology are linked through James Jesus Angleton, a high official of the Intelligence Community, to T. S. Eliot, one of his pals. Angleton, in his youth the editor of a literary magazine, had the declared aim of revitalizing the culture of the West against the 'so-to-speak Stalinists.' The ghost of T. S. Eliot, interviewed by Ginsberg on the fantail of a ship somewhere in death's waters, admits to having done little spy jobs for Angleton. Against these, the Children of Darkness, Ginsberg ranges the gurus, the bearded meditators, the poets loyal to Blake and Whitman, the 'holy creeps,' the lyrical, unsophisticated homosexuals whose little groups the secret police track on their computers, amongst whom they plant provocateurs, and whom they try to corrupt with heroin. This psychopathic vision, so touching because there is, realistically, so much to be afraid of, and also because of the hunger for goodness reflected in it, a screwball defense of beauty,

I value more than my accuser, Walish, does. I truly understand. To Ginsberg's sexual Fourth of July fireworks I say, Tee-hee. But then I muse sympathetically over his obsessions, combing my mustache downward with my fingernails, my eyes feeling keen as I try to figure him. I am a more disinterested Ginsberg admirer than Eddie is. Eddie, so to speak, comes to the table with a croupier's rake. He works for the house. He skims from poetry.

One of Walish's long-standing problems was that he looked distinctly Jewy. Certain people were distrustful and took against him with gratuitous hostility, suspecting that he was trying to pass for a full American. They'd sometimes say, as if discovering how much force it gave them to be brazen (force is always welcome), 'What was your name before it was Walish?' – a question of the type that Jews often hear. His parents were descended from north of Ireland Protestants, actually, and his mother's family name was Ballard. He signs himself Edward Ballard Walish. He pretended not to mind this. A taste of persecution made him friendly to Jews, or so he said. Uncritically delighted with his friendship, I chose to believe him.

It turns out that after many years of concealed teetering, Walish concluded that I was a fool. It was when the public began to take me seriously that he lost patience with me and his affection turned to rancor. My TV programs on music history were what did it. I can envision this – Walish watching the screen in a soiled woolen dressing gown, cupping one elbow in his hand and sucking a cigarette, assailing me while I go on about Haydn's last days, or Mozart and Salieri, developing themes on the harpsichord: 'Superstar! What a horseshit idiot!' 'Christ! How phony can you get!' 'Huckleberry Fink!'

My own name, Shawmut, had obviously been tampered with. The tampering was done long years before my father landed in America by his brother Pinye, the one who wore a pince-nez and was a music copyist for Sholom Secunda. The family must have been called Shamus or, even more degrading, Untershamus. The *untershamus*, lowest of the low in the Old World synagogue, was a quasi-unemployable incompetent and hanger-on, tangle-bearded and cursed with comic ailments like a large hernia or scrofula, a pauper's pauper. 'Orm,' as my father would say, '*auf steiffleivent*.' *Steiffleivent* was the stiff linen-and-horsehair fabric that tailors would put into the lining of a jacket to give it shape. There was nothing cheaper. 'He was so poor that he dressed in dummy cloth.' Cheaper than a shroud. But in America Shawmut turns out to be the name of a chain of banks in Massachusetts. How do you like *them* apples! You may have heard charming, appealing, sentimental things about Yiddish, but Yiddish is a *hard* language, Miss Rose. Yiddish is severe and bears down without mercy. Yes, it is often delicate, lovely, but it can be explosive as well. 'A face like a slop jar,' 'a face like a bucket of swill.' (Pig connotations give special force to Yiddish epithets.) If there is a demiurge who inspires me to speak wildly, he may have been attracted to me by this violent unsparing language.

As I tell you this, I believe that you are willingly following, and I feel the greatest affection for you. I am very much alone in Vancouver, but that is my own fault, too. When I arrived, I was invited to a party by local musicians, and I failed to please. They gave me their Canadian test for US visitors: Was I a Reaganite? I couldn't be that, but the key question was whether El Salvador might not be another Vietnam, and I lost half of the company at once by my reply: 'Nothing of the kind. The North Vietnamese are seasoned soldiers with a military tradition of many centuries – *really* tough people. Salvadorans are Indian peasants.' Why couldn't I have kept my mouth shut? What do I care about Vietnam? Two or three sympathetic guests remained, and these I drove away as follows: A professor from UBC observed that he agreed with Alexander Pope about the ultimate unreality of evil. Seen from the highest point of metaphysics. To a rational mind, nothing bad ever really happens. He was talking high-minded balls. Twaddle! I thought. I said, 'Oh? Do you mean that every gas chamber has a silver lining?'

That did it, and now I take my daily walks alone.

It is very beautiful here, with snow mountains and still harbors. Port facilities are said to be limited and freighters have to wait (at a daily fee of $10,000). To see them at anchor is pleasant. They suggest the 'Invitation au Voyage,' and also 'Anywhere, anywhere, Out of the world!' But what a clean and civilized city this is, with its clear northern waters and, beyond, the sense of an unlimited wilderness beginning where the forests bristle, spreading northward for millions of square miles and ending at ice whorls around the Pole.

Provincial academics took offense at my quirks. Too bad.

But lest it appear that I am always dishing it out, let me tell you, Miss Rose, that I have often been on the receiving end, put down by virtuosi, by artists greater than myself, in this line. The late Kippenberg, prince of musicologists, when we were at a conference in the Villa Serbelloni on Lake Como, invited me to his rooms one night to give him a preview of my paper. Well, he didn't actually invite me. I was eager. The suggestion was mine and he didn't have the heart to refuse. He was a huge man dressed in velvet dinner clothes, a copious costume, kelly green in color, upon which his large, pale, clever head seemed to have been deposited by a boom. Although he walked with two sticks, a sort of *diable boiteux*, there was no one faster with a word. He had published *the* great work on Rossini, and Rossini himself had made immortal wisecracks (like the one about Wagner: '*Il a de beaux moments mais de mauvais quarts d'heure*'). You have to imagine also the suite that Kippenberg occupied at the villa, eighteenth-century rooms, taffeta sofas, brocades, cool statuary, hot silk lamps. The servants had already shuttered the windows for the night, so the parlor was very close. Anyway, I was reading to the worldly-wise and learned Kippenberg, all swelled out in green, his long mouth agreeably composed. Funny eyes the man had, too, set at the sides of his head as if for bilateral vision, and eyebrows like caterpillars from the Tree of Knowledge. As I was reading he began to nod. I said, 'I'm afraid I'm putting you to sleep, Professor.' 'No, no – on the contrary, you're keeping me awake,' he said. That, and at my expense, was genius, and it was a privilege to have provoked it. He had been sitting, massive, with his two sticks, as if he were on a slope, skiing into profound sleep. But even at the brink, when it was being extinguished, the unique treasure of his consciousness could still dazzle. I would have gone around the world for such a put-down.

Let me, however, return to Walish for a moment. The Walishes lived in a small country house belonging to the college. It was down in the woods, which at that season were dusty. You may remember, in Florida, what New England woods are in a dry autumn – pollen, woodsmoke, decayed and mealy leaves, spiderwebs, perhaps the wing powder of dead moths. Arriving at the Walishes' stone gateposts, if we found bottles left by the milkman we'd grab them by the neck and, yelling, hurl them into the bushes. The milk was ordered for Peg Walish, who was pregnant but hated the stuff and wouldn't drink it anyway. Peg was socially above her husband. Anybody, in those days, could be; Walish had below him only Negroes and Jews, and owing to his Jewy look, was not secure even in this advantage. Bohemianism therefore gave him strength. Mrs Walish enjoyed her husband's bohemian style, or said she did. My Pergolesi and Haydn made me less objectionable to her than I might otherwise have been. Besides, I was lively company for her husband. Believe me, he needed lively company. He was depressed; his wife was worried. When she looked at me I saw the remedy-light in her eyes.

Like Alice after she had emptied the DRINK ME bottle

in Wonderland, Peg was very tall; bony but delicate, she resembled a silent-movie star named Colleen Moore, a round-eyed ingénue with bangs. In her fourth month of pregnancy, Peg was still working at Filene's, and Eddie, unwilling to get up in the morning to drive her to the station, spent long days in bed under the faded patchwork quilts. Pink, when it isn't fresh and lively, can be a desperate color. The pink of Walish's quilts sank my heart when I came looking for him. The cottage was paneled in walnut-stained boards, the rooms were sunless, the kitchen especially gloomy. I found him upstairs sleeping, his jaw undershot and his Jewish lip prominent. The impression he made was both brutal and innocent. In sleep he was bereft of the confidence into which he put so much effort. Not many of us are fully wakeful, but Walish took particular pride in being alert. That he was nobody's fool was his main premise. But in sleep he didn't look clever.

I got him up. He was embarrassed. He was not the complete bohemian after all. His muzziness late in the day distressed him, and he grumbled, putting his thin legs out of bed. We went to the kitchen and began to drink.

Peg insisted that he see a psychiatrist in Providence. He kept this from me awhile, finally admitting that he needed a tune-up, minor internal adjustments. Becoming a father rattled him. His wife eventually gave birth to male twins. The facts are trivial and I don't feel that I'm betraying a trust. Besides, I owe him nothing. His letter upset me badly. What a time he chose to send it! Thirty-five years without a cross word. He allows me to count on his affection. Then he lets me have it. When do you shaft a pal, when do you hand him the poison cup? Not while he's still young enough to recover. Walish waited till the very end – *my* end, of course. *He* is still youthful, he writes me. Evidence of this is that he takes a true interest in young lesbians out in Missouri, he alone knows their inmost hearts and they allow him to make love to them – Walish, the sole male exception. Like the explorer McGovern, who went to Lhasa in disguise, the only Westerner to penetrate the sacred precincts. They trust only youth, they trust him, so it's certain that he can't be old.

This document of his pulls me to pieces entirely. And I agree, objectively, that my character is not an outstanding success. I am inattentive, spiritually lazy, I tune out. I have tried to make this indolence of mine look good, he says. For example, I never would check a waiter's arithmetic; I refused to make out my own tax returns; I was too 'unworldly' to manage my own investments, and hired experts (read 'crooks'). Realistic Walish wasn't too good to fight over nickels; it was the principle that counted, as honor did with Shakespeare's great soldiers. When credit cards began to be used, Walish, after computing interest and service charges to the fourth decimal, cut up Peg's cards and threw them down the chute. Every year he fought it out with tax examiners, both federal and state. Nobody was going to get the better of Eddie Walish. By such hardness he connected himself with the skinflint rich – the founding Rockefeller, who wouldn't tip more than a dime, or Getty the billionaire, in whose mansion weekend guests were forced to use coin telephones. Walish wasn't being petty, he was being hard, strict, tighter than a frog's ass. It wasn't simply basic capitalism. Insofar as Walish was a Brecht fan, it was also Leninist or Stalinist hardness. And if I was, or appeared to be, misty about money, it was conceivably 'a semi-unconscious strategy,' he said. Did he mean that I was trying to stand out as a Jew who disdained the dirty dollar? Wanting to be taken for one of my betters? In other words, assimilationism? Only I never admitted that anti-Semites of any degree were my betters.

I wasn't trying to be absentmindedly angelic about my finances. In fact, Miss Rose, I was really not with it. My ineptness with money was part of the same hysterical syndrome that caused me to put my foot in my mouth. I suffered from it genuinely, and continue to suffer. The Walish of today has forgotten that when he went to a psychiatrist to be cured of sleeping eighteen hours at a stretch, I told him how well I understood his problem. To console him, I said, 'On a good day I can be acute for about half an hour, then I start to fade out and anybody can get the better of me.' I was speaking of the dream condition or state of vague turbulence in which, with isolated moments of clarity, most of us exist. And it never occurred to me to adopt a strategy. I told you before that at one time it seemed a practical necessity to have a false self, but that I soon gave up on it. Walish, however, assumes that every clever modern man is his own avant-garde invention. To be avant-garde means to tamper with yourself, to have a personal project requiring a histrionic routine – in short, to put on an act. But what sort of act was it to trust a close relative who turned out to be a felon, or to let my late wife persuade me to hand over my legal problems to her youngest brother? It was the brother-in-law who did me in. Where others were simply unprincipled and crooked, he was in addition bananas. Patience, I am getting around to that.

Walish writes, 'I thought it was time you knew what you were really like,' and gives me a going-over such as few men ever face. I abused and badmouthed everybody,

I couldn't bear that people should express themselves (this particularly irritated him; he mentions it several times) but put words into their mouths, finished their sentences for them, making them forget what they were about to say (supplied the platitudes they were groping for). I was, he says, 'a mobile warehouse of middle-class spare parts,' meaning that I was stocked with the irrelevant and actually insane information that makes the hateful social machine tick on toward the bottomless pit. And so forth. As for my supernal devotion to music, that was merely a cover. The real Shawmut was a canny promoter whose *Introduction to Music Appreciation* was adopted by a hundred colleges ('which doesn't happen of itself') and netted him a million in royalties. He compares me to Kissinger, a Jew who made himself strong in the Establishment, having no political base or constituency but succeeding through promotional genius, operating as a celebrity . . . Impossible for Walish to understand the strength of character, even the constitutional, biological force such an achievement would require; to appreciate (his fur-covered ear sunk in his pillow, and his small figure thrice-bent, like a small fire escape, under the wads of pink quilt) what it takes for an educated man to establish a position of strength among semiliterate politicians. No, the comparison is far-fetched. Doing eighteenth-century music on PBS is

not very much like taking charge of US foreign polic,
and coping with drunkards and liars in the Congress or
the executive branch.

An honest Jew? That would be Ginsberg the Confes-
sor. Concealing no fact, Ginsberg appeals to Jew-haters
by exaggerating everything that they ascribe to Jews
in their pathological fantasies. He puts them on, I
think, with crazy simple-mindedness, with his actual
dreams of finding someone's anus in his sandwich or
with his poems about sticking a dildo into himself. This
bottom-line materialistic eroticism is most attractive to
Americans, proof of sincerity and authenticity. It's on
this level that they tell you they are 'leveling' with you,
although the deformities and obscenities that come out
must of course be assigned to somebody else, some
'morphodite' faggot or exotic junkie queer. When they
tell you they're 'leveling,' put your money in your shoe
at once, that's my advice.

I see something else in Ginsberg, however. True, he's
playing a traditional Jewish role with this comic self-
degradation, just as it was played in ancient Rome, and
probably earlier. But there's something else, equally
traditional. Under all this all-revealing candor (or aggra-
vated self-battery) is purity of heart. As an American
Jew he must also affirm and justify democracy The
United States is destined to become one of the great

achievements of humanity, a nation made up of many nations (not excluding the queer nation: how can anybody be left out?). The USA itself is to be the greatest of poems, as Whitman prophesied. And the only authentic living representative of American Transcendentalism is that fat-breasted, bald, bearded homosexual in smeared goggles, innocent in his uncleanness. Purity from foulness, Miss Rose. The man is a Jewish microcosm of this Midas earth whose buried corpses bring forth golden fruits. This is not a Jew who goes to Israel to do battle with Leviticus to justify homosexuality He is a faithful faggot Buddhist in America, the land of his birth. The petrochemical capitalist enemy (an enemy that needs sexual and religious redemption) is right here at home. Who could help loving such a comedian! Besides, Ginsberg and I were born under the same birth sign, and both of us had crazy mothers and are given to inspired utterances. I, however, refuse to overvalue the erotic life. I do not believe that the path of truth must pass through all the zones of masturbation and buggery. He is consistent; to his credit, he goes all the way, which can't be said of me. Of the two of us, he is the more American. *He* is a member of the American Academy of Arts and Letters – I've never even been proposed as a candidate – and although he has suggested that some of our recent presidents were acidheads, he has never been asked to return his national prizes and medals. The more he libels them (did LBJ use LSD?), the more medals he is likely to get. Therefore I have to admit that he is closer to the American mainstream than I am. I don't even look like an American. (Nor does Ginsberg, for that matter.) Hammond, Indiana, was my birthplace (just before Prohibition my old man had a saloon there), but I might have come straight from Kiev. I certainly haven't got the build of a Hoosier – I am tall but I slouch, my buttocks are set higher than other people's, I have always had the impression that my legs are disproportionately long: it would take an engineer to work out the dynamics. Apart from Negroes and hillbillies, Hammond is mostly foreign, there are lots of Ukrainians and Finns there. These, however, look completely American, whereas I recognize features like my own in Russian church art – the compact faces, small round eyes, arched brows, and bald heads of the icons. And in highly structured situations in which champion American executive traits like prudence and discretion are required, I always lose control and I am, as Arabs say, a hostage to my tongue.

The preceding has been fun – by which I mean that I've avoided rigorous examination, Miss Rose. We need to get closer to the subject. I have to apologize to you, but there is also a mystery here (perhaps of karma, as old Mrs Gracewell suggests) that cries out for investigation. Why does anybody *say* such things as I said to you? Well, it's as if a man were to go out on a beautiful day, a day so beautiful that it pressed him incomprehensibly to *do* something, to perform a commensurate action – or else he will feel like an invalid in a wheelchair by the seashore, a valetudinarian whose nurse says, 'Sit here and watch the ripples.'

My late wife was a gentle, slender woman, quite small, built on a narrow medieval principle. She had a way of bringing together her palms under her chin when I upset her, as if she were praying for me, and her pink color would deepen to red. She suffered extremely from my fits and assumed the duty of making amends for me, protecting my reputation and persuading people that I meant no harm. She was a brunette and her complexion was fresh. Whether she owed her color to health or excitability was an open question. Her eyes were slightly extruded, but there was no deformity in this; it was one of her beauties as far as I was concerned. She was Austrian by birth (Graz, not Vienna), a refugee. I never was attracted to women of my own build – two tall persons made an incomprehensible jumble together. Also I preferred to have to search for what I wanted. As a schoolboy, I took no sexual interest in teachers. I fell in love with the smallest girl in the class, and I followed my earliest taste in marrying a slender van der Weyden or Lucas Cranach woman. The rose color was not confined to her face. There was something not exactly contemporary about her complexion, and her conception of gracefulness also went back to a former age. She had a dipping way about her: her figure dipped when she walked, her hands dipped from the wrist while she was cooking, she was a dippy eater, she dipped her head attentively when you had anything serious to tell her and opened her mouth a little to appeal to you to make better sense. In matters of principle, however irrational, she was immovably obstinate. Death has taken Gerda out of circulation, and she has been wrapped up and put away for good. No more straight, flushed body and pink breasts, nor blue extruded eyes.

What I said to you in passing the library would have appalled her. She took it to heart that I should upset people. Let me cite an example. This occurred years later, at another university (a real one), one evening when Gerda put on a dinner for a large group of academics – all three leaves were in our cherrywood Scandinavian table. I didn't even know who the guests were. After the main course, a certain Professor Schulteiss was mentioned. Schulteiss was one of those bragging polymath types who gave everybody a pain in the ass.

Whether it was Chinese cookery or particle physics or the connections of Bantu with Swahili (if any) or why Lord Nelson was so fond of William Beckford or the future of computer science, you couldn't interrupt him long enough to complain that he didn't let you get a word in edgewise. He was a big, bearded man with an assault-defying belly and fingers that turned back at the tips, so that if I had been a cartoonist I would have sketched him yodeling, with black whiskers and retroussé fingertips. One of the guests said to me that Schulteiss was terribly worried that no one would be learned enough to write a proper obituary when he died. 'I don't know if I'm qualified,' I said, 'but I'd be happy to do the job, if that would be of any comfort to him.' Mrs Schulteiss, hidden from me by Gerda's table flowers, was being helped just then to dessert. Whether she had actually heard me didn't matter, for five or six guests immediately repeated what I had said, and I saw her move aside the flowers to look at me.

In the night I tried to convince Gerda that no real harm had been done. Anna Schulteiss was not easy to wound. She and her husband were on the outs continually – why had she come without him? Besides, it was hard to guess what she was thinking and feeling; some of her particles (a reference to Schulteiss's learning in the field of particle physics) were surely out of place. This sort of comment only made matters worse. Gerda did not tell me that, but only lay stiff on her side of the bed. In the field of troubled breathing in the night she was an accomplished artist, and when she sighed heavily there was no sleeping. I yielded to the same stiffness and suffered with her. Adultery, which seldom tempted me, couldn't have caused more guilt. While I drank my morning coffee Gerda telephoned Anna Schulteiss and made a lunch date with her. Later in the week they went to a symphony concert together. Before the month was out we were baby-sitting for the Schulteisses in their dirty little university house, which they had turned into a Stone Age kitchen midden. When that stage of conciliation had been reached, Gerda felt better. My thought, however, was that a man who allowed himself to make such jokes should be brazen enough to follow through, not succumb to conscience as soon as the words were out. He should carry things off like the princely Kippenberg. Anyway, which was the real Shawmut, the man who made insulting jokes or the other one, who had married a wife who couldn't bear that anyone should be wounded by his insults?

You will ask: With a wife willing to struggle mortally to preserve you from the vindictiveness of the injured parties, weren't you perversely tempted to make trouble, just to set the wheels rolling? The answer is no, and the reason is not only that I loved Gerda (my love terribly confirmed by her death), but also that when I said things I said them for art's sake, i.e., without perversity or malice, nor as if malice had an effect like alcohol and I was made drunk on wickedness. I reject that. Yes, there has to be some provocation. But what happens when I am provoked happens because the earth heaves up underfoot, and then from opposite ends of the heavens I get a simultaneous shock to both ears. I am deafened, and I have to open my mouth. Gerda, in her simplicity, tried to neutralize the ill effects of the words that came out and laid plans to win back the friendship of all kinds of unlikely parties whose essential particles were missing and who had no capacity for friendship, no interest in it. To such people she sent azaleas, begonias, cut flowers, she took the wives to lunch. She came home and told me earnestly how many fascinating facts she had learned about them, how their husbands were underpaid, or that they had sick old parents, or madness in the family, or fifteen-year-old kids who burglarized houses or were into heroin.

I never said anything wicked to Gerda, only to provocative people. Yours is the only case I can remember where there was no provocation, Miss Rose – hence this letter of apology, the first I have ever written. You are the cause of my self-examination. I intend to get back to this later. But I am thinking now about Gerda. For her sake I tried to practice self-control, and eventually I began to learn the value of keeping one's mouth shut, and how it can give a man strength to block his inspired words and to let the wickedness (if wickedness is what it is) be absorbed into the system again. Like the 'right speech' of Buddhists, I imagine. 'Right speech' is sound physiology. And did it make much sense to utter choice words at a time when words have sunk into grossness and decadence? If a La Rochefoucauld were to show up, people would turn away from him in mid-sentence, and yawn. Who needs maxims now?

The Schulteisses were colleagues, and Gerda could work on them, she had access to them, but there were occasions when she couldn't protect me. We were, for instance, at a formal university dinner, and I was sitting beside an old woman who gave millions of dollars to opera companies and orchestras. I was something of a star that evening and wore tails, a white tie, because I had just conducted a performance of Pergolesi's *Stabat Mater*, surely one of the most moving works of the eighteenth century. You would have thought that such music had ennobled me, at least until bedtime. But no, I soon began to spoil for trouble. It was no accident that I was on Mrs Pergamon's right. She was going to be hit

for a big contribution. Somebody had dreamed up a
schola cantorum, and I was supposed to push it (tact-
fully). The real pitch would come later. Frankly, I didn't
like the fellows behind the plan. They were a bad lot,
and a big grant would have given them more power
than was good for anyone. Old Pergamon had left his
wife a prodigious fortune. So much money was almost
a sacred attribute. And also I had conducted sacred
music, so it was sacred against sacred. Mrs Pergamon
talked money to me, she didn't mention the *Stabat Mater*
or my interpretation of it. It's true that in the US, money
leads all other topics by about a thousand to one, but
this was one occasion when the music should not have
been omitted. The old woman explained to me that the
big philanthropists had an understanding, and how the
fields were divided up among Carnegie, Rockefeller,
Mellon, and Ford. Abroad there were the various Roths-
child interests and the Volkswagen Foundation. The
Pergamons did music, mainly. She mentioned the sums
spent on electronic composers, computer music, which
I detest, and I was boiling all the while that I bent a look
of perfect courtesy from Kiev on her. I had seen her lim-
ousine in the street with campus cops on guard,
supplementing the city police. The diamonds on her
bosom lay like the Finger Lakes among their hills. I am
obliged to say that the money conversation had curious

effects on me. It reached very deep places. My late brother, whose whole life was devoted to money, had been my mother's favorite. He remains her favorite still, and she is in her nineties. Presently I heard Mrs Pergamon say that she planned to write her memoirs. Then I asked – and Nietzsche might have described the question as springing from my inner *Fatum* – 'Will you use a typewriter or an adding machine?'

Should I have said *that*? Did I actually *say* it? Too late to ask, the tempest had fallen. She looked at me, quite calm. Now, she was a great lady and I was from Bedlam. Because there was no visible reaction in her diffuse old face, and the blue of her eyes was wonderfully clarified and augmented by her glasses, I was tempted to believe that she didn't hear or else had failed to understand. But that didn't wash. I changed the subject. I understood that despite the almost exclusive interest in music, she had from time to time supported scientific research. The papers reported that she had endowed a project for research in epilepsy. Immediately I tried to steer her into epilepsy. I mentioned the Freud essay in which the theory was developed that an epileptic fit was a dramatization of the death of one's father. This was why it made you stiff. But finding that my struggle to get off the hook was only giving me a bloody lip, I went for the bottom and lay there coldly silent. With all my heart I concentrated on the *Fatum*. *Fatum* signifies that in each human being there is something that is inaccessible to revision. This something can be taught *nothing*. Maybe it is founded in the Will to Power, and the Will to Power is nothing less than Being itself. Moved, or as the young would say, stoned out of my head, by the *Stabat Mater* (the glorious mother who would not stand up for *me*), I had been led to speak from the depths of my *Fatum*. I believe that I misunderstood old Mrs Pergamon entirely. To speak of money to me was kindness, even magnanimity on her part – a man who knew Pergolesi was as good as rich and might almost be addressed as an equal. And in spite of me she endowed the schola cantorum. You don't penalize an institution because a kook at dinner speaks wildly to you. She was so very old that she had seen every sort of maniac there is. Perhaps I startled myself more than I did her.

She was being gracious, Miss Rose, and I had been trying to go beyond her, to pass her on a dangerous curve. A power contest? What might that mean? Why did I need power? Well, I may have needed it because from a position of power you can say anything. Powerful men give offense with impunity. Take as an instance what Churchill said about an MP named Driberg: 'He is the man who brought pederasty into disrepute.' And Driberg instead of being outraged was flattered, so that when another member of Parliament claimed the remark for himself and insisted that his was the name Churchill had spoken, Driberg said, '*You?* Why would Winston take notice of an insignificant faggot like *you!*' This quarrel amused London for several weeks. But then Churchill was Churchill, the descendant of Marlborough, his great biographer, and also the savior of his country. To be insulted by him guaranteed your place in history. Churchill was, however, a holdover from a more civilized age. A less civilized case would be that of Stalin. Stalin, receiving a delegation of Polish Communists in the Kremlin, said, 'But what has become of that fine, intelligent woman Comrade Z?' The Poles looked at their feet. Because, as Stalin himself had had Comrade Z murdered, there was nothing to say.

This is contempt, not wit. It is Oriental despotism, straight, Miss Rose. Churchill was human, Stalin merely a colossus. As for us, here in America, we are a demotic, hybrid civilization. We have our virtues but are ignorant of style. It's only because American society has no place for style (in the sense of Voltairean or Gibbonesque style, style in the manner of Saint-Simon or Heine) that it is possible for a man like me to make such statements as he makes, harming no one but himself. If people are offended, it's by the 'hostile intent' they sense, not by the keenness of the words. They classify me then as a psychological curiosity, a warped personality. It never occurs to them to take a full or biographical view. In the real sense of the term, biography has fallen away from us. We all flutter like new-hatched chicks between the feet of the great idols, the monuments of power.

So what are words? A lawyer, the first one, the one who represented me in the case against my brother's estate (the second one was Gerda's brother) – lawyer number one, whose name was Klaussen, said to me when an important letter had to be drafted, '*You* do it, Shawmut. You're the man with the words.'

'And you're the whore with ten cunts!'

But I didn't say this. He was too powerful. I needed him. I was afraid.

But it was inevitable that I should offend him, and presently I did.

I can't tell you *why*. It's a mystery. When I tried to discuss Freud's epilepsy essay with Mrs Pergamon I wanted to hint that I myself was subject to strange seizures that resembled falling sickness. But it wasn't just brain pathology, lesions, grand mal chemistry. It was a kind of perversely happy *gaieté de coeur*. Elements of vengefulness, or blasphemy? Well, maybe. What about demonic inspiration, what about energumens, what about Dionysus the god? After a distressing luncheon with Klaussen the lawyer at his formidable club, where he bullied me in a dining room filled with bullies, a scene from Daumier (I had been beaten down ten or twelve times, my suggestions all dismissed, and I had paid him a twenty-five-thousand-dollar retainer, but Klaussen hadn't bothered yet to master the elementary facts of the case) – after lunch, I say, when we were walking through the lobby of the club, where federal judges, machine politicians, paving contractors, and chairmen of boards conferred in low voices, I heard a great noise. Workmen had torn down an entire wall. I said to the receptionist, 'What's happening?' She answered, 'The entire club is being rewired. We've been having daily power failures from the old electrical system.' I said, 'While they're at it they might arrange to have people electrocuted in the dining room.'

I was notified by Klaussen next day that for one reason or another he could no longer represent me. I was an incompatible client.

The intellect of man declaring its independence from worldly power – okay. But I had gone to Klaussen for protection. I chose him because he was big and arrogant, like the guys my brother's widow had hired. My late brother had swindled me. Did I want to recover my money or not? Was I fighting or doodling? Because in the courts you needed brazenness, it was big arrogance or nothing. And with Klaussen as with Mrs Pergamon there was not a thing that Gerda could do – she couldn't send either of them flowers or ask them to lunch. Besides, she was already sick. Dying, she was concerned about my future. She remonstrated with me. 'Did you have to needle him? He's a proud man.'

'I gave in to my weakness. What's with me? Like, am I too good to be a hypocrite?'

'Hypocrisy is a big word. . . . A little lip service.'

And again I said what I shouldn't have, especially given the state of her health: 'It's a short step from lip service to ass kissing.'

'Oh, my poor Herschel, you'll never change!'

She was then dying of leukemia, Miss Rose, and I had to promise her that I would put my case in the hands of her brother Hansl. She believed that for her sake Hansl would be loyal to me. Sure, his feeling for her was genuine. He loved his sister. But as a lawyer he was a disaster, not because he was disloyal but because he was in essence an inept conniver. Also he was plain crackers.

Lawyers, lawyers. Why did I need all these lawyers? you will ask. Because I loved my brother fondly. Because we did business, and business can't be done without lawyers. They have built a position for themselves at the very heart of money – strength at the core of what is strongest. Some of the cheerfulest passages in Walish's letter refer to my horrible litigation. He says, 'I always knew you were a fool.' Himself, he took the greatest pains never to be one. Not that any man can ever be absolutely certain that his prudence is perfect. But to retain lawyers is clear proof that you're a patsy. There I concede that Walish is right.

My brother, Philip, had offered me a business proposition, and that, too, was my fault. I made the mistake of telling him how much money my music-appreciation book had earned. He was impressed. He said to his wife, 'Tracy, guess who's loaded!' Then he asked, 'What are you doing with it? How do you protect yourself against taxes and inflation?'

I admired my brother, not because he was a 'creative businessman,' as they said in the family – that meant little to me – but because . . . Well, there is in fact no 'because,' there's only the *given*, a lifelong feeling, a mystery. His interest in my finances excited me. For once he spoke seriously to me, and this turned my head. I told him, 'I never even tried to make money, and now I'm knee-deep in the stuff.' Such a statement was a little disingenuous. It was, if you prefer, untrue. To take such a tone was also a mistake, for it implied that money wasn't so hard to make. Brother Philip had knocked himself out for it while Brother Harry had earned heaps of it, incidentally, while fiddling. This, I now acknowledge, was a provocative booboo. He made a dark note of it. I even saw the note being made.

As a boy, Philip was very fat. We had to sleep together when we were children and it was like sharing the bed with a dugong. But since then he had firmed up quite a lot. In profile his face was large, with bags under the eyes, a sharp serious face upon a stout body. My late brother was a crafty man. He laid long-distance schemes. Over me he enjoyed the supreme advantage of detachment. My weakness was my fondness for him, contemptible in an adult male. He slightly resembled Spencer Tracy, but was more avid and sharp. He had a Texas tan, his hair was 'styled,' not barbered, and he wore Mexican rings on every one of his fingers.

Gerda and I were invited to visit his estate near Houston. Here he lived in grandeur, and when he showed me around the place he said to me, 'Every morning when I open my eyes I say, "Philip, you're living right in the middle of a park. You own a whole park."'

I said, 'It certainly is as big as Douglas Park in Chicago.'

He cut me short, not wishing to hear about the old West Side, our dreary origins. Roosevelt Road with its chicken coops stacked on the sidewalks, the Talmudist horseradish grinder in the doorway of the fish store, or the daily drama of the Shawmut kitchen on Independence Boulevard. He abominated these reminiscences of mine, for he was thoroughly Americanized. On the other hand, he no more belonged on this Texas estate than I did. Perhaps no one belonged here. Numerous failed entrepreneurs had preceded him in this private park, the oilmen and land developers who had caused this monument to be built. You had the feeling that they must all have died in flophouses or on state funny farms, cursing the grandiose fata morgana that Philip now owned, or seemed to own. The truth was that he didn't like it, either; he was stuck with it. He had bought it for various symbolic reasons, and under pressure from his wife.

He told me in confidence that he had a foolproof investment for me. People were approaching him with hundreds of thousands, asking to be cut into the deal, but he would turn them all down for my sake. For once he was in a position to do something for me. Then he set his conditions. The first condition was that he was never to be questioned, that was how he did business, but I could be sure that he would protect me as a brother should and that there was nothing to fear. In the fragrant plantation gardens, he flew for one instant (no more) into Yiddish. He'd never let me lay my sound head in a sickbed. Then he flew out again. He said that his wife, who was the best woman in the world and the soul of honor, would respect his commitments and carry out his wishes with fanatical fidelity if anything were to happen to him. Her fanatical fidelity to him was fundamental. I didn't understand Tracy, he said. She was difficult to know but she was a true woman, and he wasn't going to have any clauses in our partnership agreement that would bind her formally. She would take offense at that and so would he. And you wouldn't believe, Miss Rose, how all these clichés moved me. I responded as if to an accelerator under his fat, elegantly shod foot, pumping blood, not gasoline, into my mortal engine. I was wild with feeling and said yes to it all. Yes, yes! The plan was to create an auto-wrecking center, the biggest in Texas, which would supply auto parts to the entire South and to Latin America as well. The big German and Italian exporters were notoriously short of replacement parts; I had experienced this myself – I had once had to wait four months for a BMW front-wheel stabilizer unobtainable in the US. But it wasn't the business proposition that carried me away, Miss Rose. What affected me was that my brother and I should be really associated for the first time in our lives. As our joint enterprise could never in the world be Pergolesi, it must necessarily be business. I was unreasonably stirred by emotions that had waited a lifetime for expression; they must have worked their way into my heart at a very early age, and now came out in full strength to drag me down.

'What have you got to do with wrecking automobiles?' said Gerda. 'And grease, and metal, and all that noise?'

I said, 'What has the IRS ever done for music that it should collect half my royalties?'

My wife was an educated woman, Miss Rose, and she began to reread certain books and to tell me about them, especially at bedtime. We went through much of Balzac. *Père Goriot* (what daughters can do to a father), *Cousin Pons* (how an elderly innocent was dragged down by relatives who coveted his art collection) . . . One swindling relative after another, and all of them merciless. She related the destruction of poor César Birotteau, the trusting perfumer. She also read me selections from Marx on the obliteration of the ties of kinship by capitalism. But it never occurred to me that such evils could affect a man who had read about them. I had read about venereal diseases and had never caught any. Besides, it was now too late to take a warning.

On my last trip to Texas I visited the vast, smoking wrecking grounds, and on our way back to the mansion Philip told me that his wife had become a breeder of pit bulldogs. You may have read about these creatures, which have scandalized American animal lovers. They are the most terrifying of all dogs. Part terrier, part English bulldog, smooth-skinned, broad-chested, immensely muscular, they attack all strangers, kids as well as grownups. As they do not bark, no warning is given. Their intent is always to kill, and once they have begun to tear at you they can't be called off. The police, if they arrive in time, have to shoot them. In the pit, the dogs fight and die in silence. Aficionados bet millions of dollars on the fights (which are illegal, but what of it?). Humane societies and civil liberties groups don't quite know how to defend these murderous animals or the legal rights of their owners. There is a Washington lobby trying to exterminate the breed, and meantime enthusiasts go on experimenting, doing everything possible to create the worst of all possible dogs.

Philip took an intense pride in his wife. 'Tracy is a wonder, isn't she?' he said. 'There's terrific money in these animals. Trust her to pick up a new trend. Guys are pouring in from all over the country to buy pups from her.'

He took me to the dog-runs to show the pit bulls off. As we passed, they set their paws on the wire meshes and bared their teeth. I didn't enjoy visiting the pens. My own teeth were on edge. Philip himself wasn't comfortable with the animals, by any means. He them, they were assets, but he wasn't the master. Tracy, appearing among the dogs, gave me a silent nod. The Negro employees who brought meat were tolerated. 'But Tracy,' Philip said, 'she's their goddess.'

I must have been afraid, because nothing satirical or caustic came to mind. I couldn't even make up funny impressions to take home to Gerda, with whose amusement I was preoccupied in those sad days.

But as a reverberator, which it is my nature to be, I tried to connect the breeding of these terrible dogs with the mood of the country. The pros and cons of the matter add some curious lines to the spiritual profile of the USA. Not long ago, a lady wrote to the *Boston Globe* that it had been a failure of judgment in the Founding Fathers not to consider the welfare of cats and dogs in our democracy, people being what they are. The Founders were too lenient with human viciousness, she said, and the Bill of Rights ought to have made provision for the safety of those innocents who are forced to depend upon us. The first connection to come to mind was that egalitarianism was now being extended to cats and dogs. But it's not simple egalitarianism, it's a merging of different species; the line between man and other animals is becoming blurred. A dog will give you such simple heart's truth as you will never get from a lover or a parent. I seem to recall from the thirties (or did I read this in the memoirs of Lionel Abel?) how scandalized the French Surrealist André Breton was when he visited Leon Trotsky in exile. While the two men were discussing World Revolution, Trotsky's dog came up to be caressed and Trotsky said, 'This is my only true friend.' What? A dog the friend of this Marxist theoretician and hero of the October Revolution, the organizer of the Red Army? Symbolic Surrealist acts, like shooting at random into a crowd in the street, Breton could publicly recommend, but to be sentimental about a dog like any bourgeois was shocking. Today's psychiatrists would not be shocked. Asked whom they love best, their patients reply in increasing numbers, 'My dog.' At this rate, a dog in the White House becomes a real possibility. Not a pit bulldog, certainly, but a nice golden retriever whose veterinarian would become Secretary of State.

I didn't try these reflections out on Gerda. Nor, since it would have been unsettling, did I tell her that Philip, too, was unwell. He had been seeing a doctor. Tracy had him on a physical-fitness program. Mornings he entered the annex to the master bedroom, in which the latest gymnastic equipment had been set up. Wearing overlong silk boxer shorts (I reckon that their theme was the whiskey sour, since they were decorated with orange slices resembling wheels), he hung by his fat arms from the shining apparatus, he jogged on a treadmill with an odometer, and he tugged at the weights. When he worked out on the Exercycle, the orange-slice wheels of his underpants extended the vehicular fantasy, but he was going nowhere. The queer things he found himself doing as a rich man, the false position he was in! His adolescent children were rednecks. The druidic Spanish moss vibrated to the shocks of rock music. The dogs bred for cruelty bided their time. My brother, it appeared, was only the steward of his wife and children.

Still, he wanted me to observe him at his exercises and to impress me with his strength. As he did push-ups, his dipping titties touched the floor before his chin did, but his stern face censored any comical comments I might be inclined to make. I was called upon to witness that under the fat there was a block of primal powers, a strong heart in his torso, big veins in his neck, and bands of muscle across his back. 'I can't do any of that,' I told him, and indeed I couldn't, Miss Rose. My behind is like a rucksack that has slipped its straps.

I made no comments, because I was a general partner who had invested $600,000 in the wreckage of rusty automobiles. Two miles behind the private park, there were cranes and compactors, and hundreds of acres were filled with metallic pounding and dust. I understood by now that the real power behind this enterprise was Philip's wife, a short round blonde of butch self-sufficiency, as dense as a meteorite and, somehow, as spacey, But no, it was I who was spacey, while she was intricately shrewd.

And most of my connubial ideas derived from the gentleness and solicitude of my own Gerda!

During this last visit with Brother Philip, I tried to get him to speak about Mother. The interest he took in her was minimal. Family sentiment was not his dish. All that he had was for the new family; for the old family, nix. He said he couldn't recall Hammond, Indiana, or Independence Boulevard. 'You were the only one I ever cared for,' he said. He was aware that there were two departed sisters, but their names didn't come to him. Without half trying, he was far ahead of André Breton, and could never be overtaken. Surrealism wasn't a theory, it was an anticipation of the future.

'What was Chink's real name?' he said.

I laughed. 'What, you've forgotten Helen's name? You're bluffing. Next you'll tell me you can't remember her husband, either. What about Kramm? He bought you your first pair of long pants. Or Sabina? She got you the job in the bucket shop in the Loop.'

'They fade from my mind,' he said. 'Why should I

keep those dusty memories? If I want details I can get you to fill me in. You've got such a memory hang-up – what use is it?'

As I grow older, Miss Rose, I don't dispute such views or opinions but tend instead to take them under consideration. True, I counted on Philip's memory. I wanted him to remember that we were brothers. I had hoped to invest my money safely and live on an income from wrecked cars – summers in Corsica, handy to London at the beginning of the musical season. Before the Arabs sent London real estate so high, Gerda and I discussed buying a flat in Kensington. But we waited and waited, and there was not a single distribution from the partnership. 'We're doing great,' said Philip. 'By next year I'll be able to remortgage, and then you and I will have more than a million to cut up between us. Until then, you'll have to be satisfied with the tax write-offs.'

I started to talk about our sister Chink, thinking my only expedient was to stir such family sentiments as might have survived in this atmosphere where the Spanish moss was electronicized by rock music (and, at the back, the pit bulldogs were drowning silently in the violence of their blood-instincts). I recalled that we had heard very different music on Independence Boulevard. Chink would play 'Jimmy Had a Nickel' on the piano, and the rest of us would sing the chorus, or yell it out. Did

Philip remember that Kramm, who drove a soda-pop truck (it was from affection, because he doted on Helen, that he called her Chink), could accurately pitch a case filled with bottles into a small opening at the very top of the pyramid? No, the pop truck wasn't exactly stacked like a pyramid, it was a ziggurat.

'What's a ziggurat?'

Assyrian or Babylonian, I explained, terraced, and not coming to a peak.

Philip said, 'Sending you to college was a mistake, although I don't know what else you would have been fit for. Nobody else went past high school . . . Kramm was okay, I guess.'

Yes, I said, Chink got Kramm to pay my college tuition. Kramm had been a doughboy, did Philip remember that? Kramm was squat but powerful, full-faced, smooth-skinned like a Samoan, and wore his black hair combed flat to his head in the Valentino or George Raft style. He supported us all, paid the rent. Our dad, during the Depression, was peddling carpets to farm women in northern Michigan. *He* couldn't earn the rent. From top to bottom, the big household became Mother's responsibility, and if she had been a little tetched before, melodramatic, in her fifties she seemed to become crazed. There was something military about the way she took charge of the house. Her command post was the kitchen. Kramm had to be fed because he fed us, and he was an enormous eater. She cooked tubs of stuffed cabbage and of chop suey for him. He could swallow soup by the bucket, put down an entire pineapple upside-down cake by himself. Mother shopped, peeled, chopped, boiled, fried, roasted, and baked, served and washed. Kramm ate himself into a stupor and then, in the night, he might come out in his pajama bottoms, walking in his sleep. He went straight to the icebox. I recalled a summer's night when I watched him cutting oranges in half and ripping into them with his teeth. In his somnambulism he slurped away about a dozen of them, and then I saw him go back to bed, following his belly to the right door.

'And gambled in a joint called the Diamond Horseshoe, Kedzie and Lawrence,' said Philip. He did not, however, intend to be drawn into any reminiscences. He began, a little, to smile, but he remained basically gloomy, reserved.

Of course. He had entered upon one of his biggest swindles.

He changed the subject. He asked if I didn't admire the way Tracy ran this large estate. She was a magician. She didn't need interior decorators, she had done the whole place by herself. All the linens were Portuguese. The gardens were wonderful. Her roses won prizes.

The appliances never gave trouble. She was a cordon bleu cook. It was true the kids were difficult, but that was how kids were nowadays. She was a terrific psychologist, and fundamentally the little bastards were well adjusted. They were just American youngsters. His greatest satisfaction was that everything was so American. It was, too – an all-American production.

For breakfast, if I called the kitchen persistently, I could have freeze-dried coffee and a slice of Wonder bread. They were brought to my room by a black person who answered no questions. Was there an egg, a piece of toast, a spoonful of jam? Nothing. It wounds me desperately not to be fed. As I sat waiting for the servant to come with the freeze-dried coffee and the absorbent-cotton bread, I prepared and polished remarks that I might make to her, considering how to strike a balance between satire and human appeal. It was a waste of time to try to reach a common human level with the servants. It was obvious that I was a guest of no importance, Miss Rose. No one would listen. I could almost hear the servants being instructed to 'come slack of former services' or 'Put on what weary negligence you please' – the words of Goneril in *King Lear*. Also the room they had given me had been occupied by one of the little girls, now too big for it. The wallpaper, illustrated with Simple Simon and Goosey

Gander, at the time seemed inappropriate (it now seems sharply pertinent).

And I was obliged to listen to my brother's praise of his wife. Again and again he told me how wise and good she was, how clever and tender a mother, what a brilliant hostess, respected by the best people who owned the largest estates. And a shrewd counselor. (I could believe that!) Plus a warm sympathizer when he was anxious, an energetic lover, and she gave him what he had never had before – peace. And I, Miss Rose, with $600,000 sunk here, was constrained to go along, nodding like a dummy. Forced to underwrite all of his sustaining falsehoods, countersigning the bill of goods he sold himself, I muttered the words he needed to finish his sentences. (How Walish would have jeered!) Death breathing over both the odd brothers with the very fragrance of subtropical air – magnolia, honeysuckle, orange blossom, or whatever the hell it was, puffing into our faces. Oddest of all was Philip's final confidence (untrue!). For my ears only, he whispered in Yiddish that our sisters had shrieked like *papagayas* (parrots), that for the first time in his life he had quiet here, domestic tranquillity. Not true. There was amplified rock music.

After this lapse, he reversed himself with a vengeance. For a family dinner, we drove in two Jaguars to a Chinese restaurant, a huge showplace constructed in circles, or dining wells, with tables highlighted like symphonic kettledrums. Here Philip made a scene. He ordered far too many hors d'oeuvres, and when the table was jammed with dishes he summoned the manager to complain that he was being hustled, he hadn't asked for double portions of all these fried wontons, egg rolls, and barbecued ribs. And when the manager refused to take them back Philip went from table to table with egg rolls and ribs, saying, 'Here! Free! Be my guest!' Restaurants always did excite him, but this time Tracy called him to order. She said, 'Enough, Philip, we're here to eat, not raise everybody's blood pressure.' Yet a few minutes later he pretended that he had found a pebble in his salad. I had seen this before. He carried a pebble in his pocket for the purpose. Even the kids were on to him, and one of them said, 'He's always doing this routine, Uncle.' It gave me a start to have them call me Uncle.

Indulge me for a moment, Miss Rose. I am covering the ground as quickly as I can. There's not a soul to talk to in Vancouver except ancient Mrs Gracewell, and with her I have to ride in esoteric clouds. Pretending that he had cracked his tooth, Philip had shifted from the Americanism of women's magazines (lovely wife, beautiful home, the highest standard of normalcy) to that of the rednecks – yelling at the Orientals, ordering his children to get his lawyer on the table telephone. The philistine idiosyncrasy of the rich American brute. But you can no longer be a philistine without high sophistication, matching the sophistication of what you hate. However, it's no use talking about 'false consciousness' or any of that baloney. Philly had put himself into Tracy's hands for full Americanization. To achieve this (obsolete) privilege, he paid the price of his soul. But then he may never have been absolutely certain that there is any such thing as a soul. What he resented about me was that I wouldn't stop hinting that souls existed. What was I, a Reform rabbi or something? Except at a funeral service, Philip wouldn't have put up with Pergolesi for two minutes. And wasn't I – never mind Pergolesi – looking for a hot investment?

When Philip died soon afterward, you may have read in the papers that he was mixed up with chop-shop operators in the Midwest, with thieves who stole expensive cars and tore them apart for export piecemeal to Latin America and the whole of the third world. Chop shops, however, were not Philip's crime. On the credit established by my money, the partnership acquired and resold land, but much of the property lacked clear title, there were liens against it. Defrauded purchasers brought suit. Big trouble followed. Convicted, Philip appealed, and then he jumped bail and escaped to

Mexico. There he was kidnapped while jogging in Chapultepec Park. His kidnappers were bounty hunters. The bonding companies he had left holding the bag when he skipped out had offered a bounty for his return. Specialists exist who will abduct people, Miss Rose, if the sums are big enough to make the risks worthwhile. After Philip was brought back to Texas, the Mexican government began extradition proceedings on the ground that he was snatched illegally, which he was, certainly. My poor brother died while doing push-ups in a San Antonio prison yard during the exercise hour. Such was the end of his picturesque struggles.

After we had mourned him, and I took measures to recover my losses from his estate, I discovered that his personal estate was devoid of assets. He had made all his wealth over to his wife and children.

I could not be charged with Philip's felonies, but since he had made me a general partner I was sued by the creditors. I retained Mr Klaussen, whom I lost by the remark I made in the lobby of his club about electrocuting people in the dining room. The joke was harsh, I admit, although no harsher than what people often think, but nihilism, too, has its no-nos, and professional men can't allow their clients to make such cracks. Klaussen drew the line. Thus I found myself after Gerda's death in the hands of her energetic but unbalanced brother, Hansl. He decided, on sufficient grounds, that I was an incompetent, and as he is a believer in fast action, he took dramatic measures and soon placed me in my present position. Some position! Two brothers in flight, one to the south, the other northward and faced with extradition. No bonding company will set bounty hunters on me. I'm not worth it to them. And even though Hansl had promised that I would be safe in Canada, he didn't bother to check the law himself. One of his student clerks did it for him, and since she was a smart, sexy girl it didn't seem necessary to review her conclusions.

Knowledgeable sympathizers when they ask who represents me are impressed when I tell them. They say, 'Hansl Genauer? Real smart fellow. You ought to do all right.'

Hansl dresses very sharply, in Hong Kong suits and shirts. A slender man, he carries himself like a concert violinist and has a manner that, as a manner, is fully convincing. For his sister's sake ('She had a wonderful life with you, she said to the last'), he was, or intended to be, my protector. I was a poor old guy, bereaved, incompetent, accidentally prosperous, foolishly trusting, thoroughly swindled. 'Your brother fucked you but good. He and his wife.'

'She was a party to it?'

'Try giving it a little thought. Has she answered any of your letters?'

'No.'

Not a single one, Miss Rose.

'Let me tell you how I reconstruct it, Harry,' said Hansl. 'Philip wanted to impress his wife. He was scared of her. Out of terror, he wanted to make her rich. She told him she was all the family he needed. To prove that he believed her, he had to sacrifice his old flesh and blood to the new flesh and blood. Like, "I give you the life of your dreams, all you have to do is cut your brother's throat." He did his part, he piled up dough, dough, and more dough – I don't suppose he liked you anyway – and he put all the loot in her name. So that when he died, which was *never* going to happen . . .'

Cleverness is Hansl's instrument; he plays it madly, bowing it with elegance as if he were laying out the structure of a sonata, phrase by phrase, for his backward brother-in-law. What did I need with his fiddling? Isn't there anybody, dear God, on *my* side? My brother picked me up by the trustful affections as one would lift up a rabbit by the ears. Hansl, now in charge of the case, analyzed the betrayal for me, down to the finest fibers of its brotherly bonds, and this demonstrated that he was completely on my side – right? He examined the books of the partnership, which I had never bothered to do, pointing out Philip's misdeeds. 'You see? He was leasing land from his wife, the nominal owner, for use by the wrecking company, and every year that pig paid himself a rent of ninety-eight thousand dollars. There went your profits. More deals of the same kind all over these balance sheets. While you were planning summers in Corsica.'

'I wasn't cut out for business. I see that.'

'Your dear brother was a full-time con artist. He might have started a service called Dial-a-Fraud. But then you also provoke people. When Klaussen handed over your files to me, he told me what offensive, wicked things you said. He then decided he couldn't represent you anymore.'

'But he didn't return the unused part of the fat retainer I gave him.'

'*I'll* be looking out for you now. Gerda's gone, and that leaves me to see that things don't get worse – the one adult of us three. My clients who are the greatest readers are always in the biggest trouble. What they call culture, if you ask me, causes mostly confusion and stunts their development. I wonder if you'll ever understand why you let your brother do you in the way he did.'

Philip's bad world borrowed me for purposes of its own. I had, however, approached him in the expectation of benefits, Miss Rose. I wasn't blameless. And if he and his people – accountants, managers, his wife – forced me to feel what they felt, colonized me with their realities, even with their daily moods, saw to it that I should suffer everything they had to suffer, it was after all *my* idea. I tried to make use of *them*.

I never again saw my brother's wife, his children, nor the park they lived in, nor the pit bulldogs.

'That woman is a legal genius,' said Hansl.

Hansl said to me, 'You'd better transfer what's left, your trust account, to my bank, where I can look after it. I'm on good terms with the officers over there. The guys are efficient, and no monkey business. You'll be taken care of.'

I had been taken care of before, Miss Rose. Walish was dead right about 'the life of feeling' and the people who lead it. Feelings are dreamlike, and dreaming is usually done in bed. Evidently I was forever looking for a safe place to lie down. Hansl offered to make secure arrangements for me so that I wouldn't have to wear myself out with finance and litigation, which were too stressful and labyrinthine and disruptive; so I accepted his proposal and we met with an officer of his bank. Actually the bank looked like a fine old institution, with Oriental rugs, heavy carved furniture, nineteenth-century paintings, and dozens of square acres of financial atmosphere above us. Hansl and the vice president who was going to take care of me began with small talk about the commodity market, the capers over at City Hall, the prospects for the Chicago Bears, intimacies with a couple of girls in a Rush Street bar. I saw that Hansl badly needed the points he was getting for bringing in my account. He wasn't doing well. Though nobody was supposed to say so, I was soon aware of it. Many forms were put before me, which I signed. Then two final cards were laid down just as my signing momentum seemed irreversible. But I applied the brake. I asked the vice president what these were for and he said, 'If you're busy, or out of town, these will give Mr Genauer the right to trade for you – buy or sell stocks for your account.'

I slipped the cards into my pocket, saying that I'd take them home with me and mail them in. We passed to the next item of business.

Hansl made a scene in the street, pulling me away from the great gates of the bank and down a narrow Loop alley. Behind the kitchen of a hamburger joint he let me have it. He said, 'You humiliated me.'

I said, 'We didn't discuss a power of attorney beforehand. You took me by surprise, completely. Why did you spring it on me like that?'

'You're accusing me of trying to pull a fast one? If you weren't Gerda's husband I'd tell you to beat it. You undermined me with a business associate. You weren't like this with your own brother, and I'm closer to you by affection than he was by blood, you nitwit. I wouldn't have traded your securities without notifying you.'

He was tearful with rage.

'For God's sake, let's move away from this kitchen ventilator,' I said. 'I'm disgusted with these fumes.'

He shouted, 'You're out of it! Out!'

'And you're *in* it.'

'Where the hell else is there to be?'

Miss Rose, you have understood us, I am sure of it. We were talking about the vortex. A nicer word for it is the French one, *le tourbillon*, or whirlwind. I was not out of it, it was only my project to *get* out. It's been a case of disorientation, my dear. I know that there's a right state for each of us. And as long as I'm not in the right state, the state of vision I was meant or destined to be in, I must assume responsibility for the unhappiness others suffer because of my disorientation. Until this ends there can only be errors. To put it another way, my dreams of orientation or true vision taunt me by suggesting that the world in which I – together with others – live my life is a fabrication, an amusement park that, however, does not amuse. It resembles, if you are following, my brother's private park, which was supposed to prove by external signs that he made his way into the very center of the real. Philip had prepared the setting, paid for by embezzlement, but he had nothing to set in it. He was forced to flee, pursued by bounty hunters who snatched him in Chapultepec, and so forth. At his weight, at that altitude, in the smog of Mexico City, to jog was suicidal.

Now Hansl explained himself, for when I said to him, 'Those securities can't be traded anyway. Don't you see? The plaintiffs have legally taken a list of all my holdings,' he was ready for me. 'Bonds, mostly,' he said. 'That's just where I can outfox them. They copied that list two weeks ago, and now it's in their lawyers' file and they won't check it for months to come. They think they've got you, but here's what we do: we sell those old bonds off and buy new ones to replace them. We change all the numbers. All it costs you is brokerage fees. Then, when the time comes, they find out that what they've got sewed up is bonds you no longer own. How are they going to trace the new numbers? And by then I'll have you out of the country.'

Here the skin of my head became intolerably tight, which meant even deeper error, greater horror anticipated. And, at the same time, temptation. People had kicked the hell out of me with, as yet, no reprisals. My thought was: It's time *I* made a bold move. We were in the narrow alley between two huge downtown institutions (the hamburger joint was crammed in tight). An armored Brink's truck could hardly have squeezed between the close colossal black walls.

'You mean I substitute new bonds for the old, and I can sell from abroad if I want to?'

Seeing that I was beginning to appreciate the exquisite sweetness of his scheme, Hansl gave a terrific smile and said, 'And you will. That's the dough you'll live on.'

'That's a dizzy idea,' I said.

'Maybe it is, but do you want to spend the rest of your life battling in the courts? Why not leave the country and live abroad quietly on what's left of your assets? Pick a place where the dollar is strong and spend the rest of your life in musical studies or what you goddamn well please. Gerda, God bless her, is gone. What's to keep you?'

'Nobody but my old mother.'

'Ninety-four years old? And a vegetable? You can put your textbook copyright in her name and the income will take care of her. So our next step is to check out some international law. There's a sensational chick in my office. She was on the *Yale Law Journal*. They don't come any smarter. She'll find you a country. I'll have her do a report on Canada. What about British Columbia, where old Canadians retire?'

'Whom do I know there? Whom will I talk to? And what if the creditors keep after me?'

'You haven't got so much dough left. There isn't all that much in it for them. They'll forget you.'

I told Hansl I'd consider his proposal. I had to go and visit Mother in the nursing home.

The home was decorated with the intention of making everything seem normal. Her room was much like any hospital room, with plastic ferns and fireproof drapes. The chairs, resembling wrought-iron garden furniture, were also synthetic and light. I had trouble with the ferns. I disliked having to touch them to see if they were real. It was a reflection on my relation to reality that I couldn't tell at a glance. But then Mother didn't know me, either, which was a more complex matter than the ferns.

I preferred to come at mealtimes, for she had to be fed. To feed her was infinitely meaningful for me. I took over from the orderly. I had long given up telling her, 'This is Harry.' Nor did I expect to establish rapport by feeding her. I used to feel that I had inherited something of her rich crazy nature and love of life, but it now was useless to think such thoughts. The tray was brought and the orderly tied her bib. She willingly swallowed the cream of carrot soup. When I encouraged her, she nodded. Recognition, nil. Two faces from ancient Kiev, similar bumps on the forehead. Dressed in her hospital gown, she wore a thread of lipstick on her mouth. The chapped skin of her cheeks gave her color also. By no means silent, she spoke of her family, but I was not mentioned.

'How many children have you got?' I said.

'Three: two daughters and a son, my son Philip.'

All three were dead. Maybe she was already in communication with them. There was little enough of reality remaining in this life; perhaps they had made connections in another. In the census of the living, I wasn't counted.

'My son Philip is a clever businessman.'

'Oh, I know.'

She stared, but did not ask how I knew. My nod seemed to tell her that I was a fellow with plenty of contacts, and that was enough for her.

'Philip is very rich,' she said.

'Is he?'

'A millionaire, and a wonderful son. He always used to give me money. I put it into Postal Savings. Have you got children?'

'No, I haven't.'

'My daughters come to see me. But best of all is my son. He pays all my bills.'

'Do you have friends in this place?'

'Nobody. And I don't like it. I hurt all the time, especially my hips and legs. I have so much misery that there are days when I think I should jump from the window.'

'But you won't do that, will you?'

'Well, I think: What would Philip and the girls do with a mother a cripple?'

I let the spoon slip into the soup and uttered a high laugh. It was so abrupt and piercing that it roused her to examine me.

Our kitchen on Independence Boulevard had once been filled with such cockatoo cries, mostly feminine. In the old days the Shawmut women would sit in the kitchen while giant meals were cooked, tubs of stuffed cabbage, slabs of brisket. Pineapple cakes glazed with brown sugar came out of the oven. There were no low voices there. In that cage of birds you couldn't make yourself heard if you didn't shriek, too, and I had learned as a kid to shriek with the rest, like one of those operatic woman-birds. That was what Mother now heard from me, the sound of one of her daughters. But I had no bouffant hairdo, I was bald and wore a mustache, and there was no eyeliner on my lids. While she stared at me I dried her face with the napkin and continued to feed her.

'Don't jump, Mother, you'll hurt yourself.'

But everyone here called her Mother; there was nothing personal about it.

She asked me to switch on the TV set so that she could watch *Dallas*.

I said it wasn't time yet, and I entertained her by singing snatches of the *Stabat Mater*. I sang, '*Eja mater, fonsamo-o-ris.*' Pergolesi's sacred chamber music (different from his formal masses for the Neapolitan church) was not to her taste. Of course I loved my mother, and she had once loved me. I well remember having my hair washed with a bulky bar of castile soap and how pained she was when I cried from the soap in my eyes. When she dressed me in a pongee suit (short pants of Chinese silk) to send me off to a surprise party, she kissed me ecstatically. These were events that might have occurred just before the time of the Boxer Rebellion or in the back streets of Siena six centuries ago. Bathing, combing, dressing, kissing – these now are remote antiquities. There was, as I grew older, no way to sustain them.

When I was in college (they sent me to study electrical engineering but I broke away into music) I used to enjoy saying, when students joked about their families, that because I was born just before the Sabbath, my mother was too busy in the kitchen to spare the time and my aunt had to give birth to me.

I kissed the old girl – she felt lighter to me than wickerwork. But I wondered what I had done to earn this oblivion, and why fat-assed Philip the evildoer should have been her favorite, the true son. Well, he didn't lie to her about *Dallas*, or try for his own sake to resuscitate her emotions, to appeal to her maternal memory with Christian music (fourteenth-century Latin of J. da Todi). My mother, two-thirds of her erased, and my brother – who knew where his wife had buried him? – had both been true to the present American world and its liveliest material interests. Philip therefore spoke to her understanding. I did not. By waving my long arms, conducting Mozart's *Great Mass* or Handel's *Solomon*, I wafted myself away into the sublime. So for many years I had not made sense, had talked strangely to my mother. What had she to remember me by? Half a century ago I had refused to enter into *her* kitchen performance. She had belonged to the universal regiment of Stanislavski mothers. During the twenties and thirties those women were going strong in thousands of kitchens across the civilized world from Salonika to San Diego. They had warned their daughters that the men they married would be rapists to whom they must submit in duty. And when I told her that I was going to marry Gerda, Mother opened her purse and gave me three dollars, saying, 'If you need it so bad, go to a whorehouse.' Nothing but histrionics, of course.

'Realizing how we suffer,' as Ginsberg wrote in 'Kaddish,' I was wickedly tormented. I had come to make a decision about Ma, and it was possible that I was fiddling with the deck, stacking the cards, telling myself, Miss Rose, 'It was always me that took care of this freaked-in-the-brain, afflicted, calamitous, shrill old mother, not Philip. Philip was too busy building himself up into an imperial American.' Yes, that was how I put it, Miss Rose, and I went even further. The consummation of Philip's upbuilding was to torpedo me. He got me under the waterline, a direct hit, and my fortunes exploded, a sacrifice to Tracy and his children. And now I'm supposed to be towed away for salvage.

I'll tell you the truth, Miss Rose, I was maddened by injustice. I think you'd have to agree not only that I'd been had but that I was singularly foolish, a burlesque figure. I could have modeled Simple Simon for the nursery-rhyme wallpaper of the little girl's room in Texas.

As I was brutally offensive to you without provocation, these disclosures, the record of my present state, may gratify you. Almost any elderly person, chosen at random, can provide such gratification to those he has offended. One has only to see the list of true facts, the painful inventory. Let me add, however, that while I, too, have reason to feel vengeful, I haven't experienced a Dionysian intoxication of vengefulness. In fact I have had feelings of increased calm and of enhanced strength – my emotional development has been steady, not fitful.

The Texas partnership, what was left of it, was being administered by my brother's lawyer, who answered all my inquiries with computer printouts. There were capital gains, only on paper, but I was obliged to pay taxes on them, too. The $300,000 remaining would be used up in litigation, if I stayed put, and so I decided to follow Hansl's plan even if it led to the *Götterdämmerung* of my remaining assets. All the better for your innocence and peace of mind if you don't understand these explanations. Time to hit back, said Hansl. His crafty looks were a study. That a man who was able to look so crafty shouldn't *really* be a genius of intrigue was the most unlikely thing in the world. His smiling wrinkles of deep cunning gave me confidence in Hansl. The bonds that the plaintiffs (creditors) had recorded were secretly traded for new ones. My tracks were covered, and I took off for Canada, a foreign country in which my own language, or something approaching it, is spoken. There I was to conclude my life in peace, and at an advantageous rate of exchange. I have developed a certain sympathy with Canada. It's no easy thing to share a border with the USA. Canada's chief entertainment – it has no choice – is to watch (from a gorgeous setting) what happens in our country. The disaster is that there is no other show. Night after night they sit in darkness and watch us on the lighted screen.

'Now that you've made your arrangements, I can tell you,' said Hansl, 'how proud I am that you're hitting back. To go on taking punishment from those pricks would be a disgrace.'

Busy Hansl really was crackers, and even before I took off for Vancouver I began to see that. I told myself that his private quirks didn't extend to his professional life. But before I fled, he came up with half a dozen unsettling ideas of what I had to do for him. He was a little bitter because, he said, I hadn't let him make use of my cultural prestige. I was puzzled and asked for an example. He said that for one thing I had never offered to put him up for membership in the University Club. I had had him to lunch there and it turned out that he was deeply impressed by the Ivy League class, the dignity of the bar, the leather seats, and the big windows of the dining room, decorated with the seals of the great universities in stained glass. He had graduated from De Paul, in Chicago. He had expected me to ask whether he'd like to join, but I had been too selfish or too snobbish to do that. Since he was now saving me, the least I could do was to use my influence with the membership committee. I saw his point and nominated him willingly, even with relish.

He next asked me to help him with one of his ladies. 'They're Kenwood people, an old mail-order-house fortune. The family is musical and artistic. Babette is an attractive widow. The first guy had the Big C, and to tell the truth I'm a little nervous of getting in behind him, but I can fight that. I don't think I'll catch it, too. Now, Babette is impressed by you, she's heard you conduct and read some of your music criticism, watched you on Channel Eleven. Educated in Switzerland, knows languages, and this is a case where I can use your cultural clout. What I suggest is that you take us to Les Nomades – private dining without crockery noise. I gave her the best Italian food in town at the Roman Rooftop, but they not only bang the dishes there, they poisoned her with the sodium glutamate on the veal. So feed us at the Nomades. You can deduct the amount of the tab from my next bill. I always believed that the class you impressed people with you picked up from my sister. After all, you were a family of Russian peddlers and your brother was a lousy felon. My sister not only loved you, she taught you some style. Someday it'll be recognized that if that goddamn Roosevelt hadn't shut the doors on Jewish refugees from Germany, this country wouldn't be in such trouble today. We could have had ten Kissingers, and nobody will ever know how much scientific talent went up in smoke at the camps.'

Well, at Les Nomades I did it again, Miss Rose. On the eve of my flight I was understandably in a state. Considered as a receptacle, I was tilted to the pouring point. The young widow he had designs on was attractive in ways that you had to come to terms with. It was fascinating to me that anybody with a Hapsburg lip could speak so rapidly, and I would have said that she was a little uncomfortably tall. Gerda, on whom my taste was formed, was a short, delicious woman. However, there was no reason to make comparisons.

When there are musical questions I always try earnestly to answer them. People have told me that I am comically woodenheaded in this respect, a straight man. Babette had studied music, her people were patrons of the Lyric Opera, but after she had asked for my opinion on the production of Monteverdi's *Coronation of Poppaea*, she took over, answering all her own questions. Maybe her recent loss had made her nervously talkative. I am always glad to let somebody else carry the conversation, but this Babette, in spite of her big underlip, was too much for me. A relentless talker, she repeated for

half an hour what she had heard from influential relatives about the politics surrounding cable-TV franchises
in Chicago. She followed this up with a long conversation on films. I seldom go to the movies. My wife had
no taste for them. Hansl, too, was lost in all this discus-
sion about directors, actors, new developments in the
treatment of the relations between the sexes, the pro-
gress of social and political ideas in the evolution of the
medium. I had nothing at all to say. I thought about
death, and also about the best topics for reflection
appropriate to my age, the on the whole agreeable
openness of things toward the end of the line, the out-
skirts of the City of Life. I didn't too much mind
Babette's chatter, I admired her taste in clothing, the
curved white and plum stripes of her enchanting blouse
from Bergdorf's. She was well set up. Conceivably her
shoulders were too heavy, proportional to the Hapsburg
lip. It wouldn't matter to Hansl; he was thinking about
Brains wedded to Money.

I hoped I wouldn't have a stroke in Canada. There
would be no one to look after me, neither a discreet,
gentle Gerda nor a gabby Babette.

I wasn't aware of the approach of one of my seizures, but when we were at the half-open door of the
checkroom and Hansl was telling the attendant that
the lady's coat was a three-quarter-length sable wrap,

Babette said, 'I realize now that I monopolized the conversation, I talked and talked all evening. I'm so sorry . . .'

'That's all right,' I told her. 'You didn't say a thing.'

You, Miss Rose, are in the best position to judge the effects of such a remark.

Hansl next day said to me, 'You just can't be trusted, Harry, you're a born betrayer. I was feeling sorry for you, having to sell your car and furniture and books, and about your brother who shafted you, and your old mother, and my poor sister passing, but you have no gratitude or consideration in you. You insult everybody.'

'I didn't realize that I was going to hurt the lady's feelings.'

'I could have married the woman. I had it wrapped up. But I was an idiot. I had to bring *you* into it. And now, let me tell you, you've made one more enemy.'

'Who, Babette?'

Hansl did not choose to answer. He preferred to lay a heavy, ambiguous silence on me. His eyes, narrowing and dilating with his discovery of my wicked habit, sent daft waves toward me. The message of those waves was that the foundations of his goodwill had been wiped out. In all the world, I had had only Hansl to turn to. Everybody else was estranged. And now I couldn't count on him, either. It was not a happy development for me, Miss Rose. I can't say that it didn't bother me, although I could no longer believe in my brother-in-law's dependability. By the standards of stability at the strong core of American business society, Hansl himself was a freak. Quite apart from his disjunctive habits of mind, he was disqualified by the violinist's figure he cut, the noble hands and the manicured filbert fingernails, his eyes, which were like the eyes you glimpse in the heated purple corners of the small-mammal house that reproduces the gloom of nocturnal tropics. Would any Aramco official have become his client? Hansl had no reasonable plans but only crafty fantasies, restless schemes. They puffed out like a lizard's throat and then collapsed like bubble gum.

As for insults, I never intentionally insulted anyone. I sometimes think that I don't have to say a word for people to be insulted by me, that my existence itself insults them. I come to this conclusion unwillingly, for God knows that I consider myself a man of normal social instincts and am not conscious of any will to offend. In various ways I have been trying to say this to you, using words like seizure, rapture, demonic possession, frenzy, *Fatum*, divine madness, or even solar storm – on a microcosmic scale. The better people are, the less they take offense at this gift, or curse, and I have a hunch that you will judge me less harshly than Walish. He, however, is right in one respect. You did nothing to offend me. You were the meekest, the only one of those I wounded whom I had no reason whatsoever to wound. That's what grieves me most of all. But there is still more. The writing of this letter has been the occasion of important discoveries about myself, so I am even more greatly in your debt, for I see that you have returned me good for the evil I did you. I opened my mouth to make a coarse joke at your expense and thirty-five years later the result is a communion.

But to return to what I literally am: a basically unimportant old party, ailing, cut off from all friendships, scheduled for extradition, and with a future of which the dimmest view is justified (shall I have an extra bed put in my mother's room and plead illness and incompetency?).

Wandering about Vancouver this winter, I have considered whether to edit an anthology of sharp sayings. Make my fate pay off. But I am too demoralized to do it. I can't pull myself together. Instead, fragments of things read or remembered come to me persistently while I go back and forth between my house and the supermarket. I shop to entertain myself, but Canadian supermarkets unsettle me. They aren't organized the way ours are. They carry fewer brands. Items like lettuce and bananas are priced out of sight while luxuries like frozen salmon are comparatively cheap. But how would I cope with a big frozen salmon? I couldn't fit it into my oven, and how, with arthritic hands, could I saw it into chunks?

Persistent fragments, inspired epigrams, or spontaneous expressions of ill will come and go. Clemenceau saying about Poincaré that he was a hydrocephalic in patent-leather boots. Or Churchill answering a question about the queen of Tonga as she passes in a barouche during the coronation of Elizabeth II: 'Is that small gentleman in the admiral's uniform the queen's consort?' 'I believe he is her lunch.'

Disraeli on his deathbed, informed that Queen Victoria has come to see him and is in the anteroom, says to his manservant, 'Her Majesty only wants me to carry a message to dear Albert.'

Such items might be delicious if they were not so persistent and accompanied by a despairing sense that I am no longer in control.

'You look pale and exhausted, Professor X.'

'I've been exchanging ideas with Professor Y, and I feel absolutely drained.'

Worse than this is the nervous word game I am unable to stop playing.

'She is the woman who put the "dish" into "fiendish."'
'He is the man who put the "rat" into "rational."'
'The "fruit" in "fruitless."'
'The "con" in "icon."'

Recreations of a crumbling mind, Miss Rose. Symptoms perhaps of high blood pressure, or minor tokens of private resistance to the giant public hand of the law (that hand will be withdrawn only when I am dead).

No wonder, therefore, that I spend so much time with old Mrs Gracewell. In her ticktock Meissen parlor with its uncomfortable chairs I am at home. Forty years a widow and holding curious views, she is happy in my company. Few visitors want to hear about the Divine Spirit, but I am seriously prepared to ponder the mysterious and intriguing descriptions she gives. The Divine Spirit, she tells me, has withdrawn in our time from the outer, visible world. You can see what it once wrought, you are surrounded by its created forms. But although natural processes continue, Divinity has absented itself. The wrought work is brightly divine but Divinity is not now active within it. The world's grandeur is fading. And this is our human setting, devoid of God, she says with great earnestness. But in this deserted beauty man himself still lives as a God-pervaded being. It will be up to him – to us – to bring back the light that has gone from these molded likenesses, if we are not prevented by the forces of darkness. Intellect, worshipped by all, brings us as far as natural science, and this science, although very great, is incomplete. Redemption from *mere* nature is the work of feeling and of the awakened eye of the Spirit. The body, she says, is subject to the forces of gravity. But the soul is ruled by levity, pure.

I listen to this and have no mischievous impulses. I shall miss the old girl. After much monkey business, dear Miss Rose, I am ready to listen to words of ultimate seriousness. There isn't much time left. The federal marshal, any day now, will be setting out from Seattle.

a little history

Penguin Modern Classics were launched in 1961, and have been shaping the reading habits of generations ever since.

The list began with distinctive grey spines and evocative pictorial covers – a look that, after various incarnations, continues to influence their current design – and with books that are still considered landmark classics today.

Penguin Modern Classics have caused scandal and political change, inspired great films and broken down barriers, whether social, sexual or the boundaries of language itself. They remain the most provocative, groundbreaking, exciting and revolutionary works of the last 100 years (or so).

In 2011, on the fiftieth anniversary of the Modern Classics, we're publishing fifty Mini Modern Classics: the very best short fiction by writers ranging from Beckett to Conrad, Nabokov to Saki, Updike to Wodehouse. Though they don't take long to read, they'll stay with you long after you turn the final page.